Kristoff's Crystal Adventure

By Apple Jordan

Illustrated by the Disney Storybook Art Team

g A GOLDEN BOOK • NEW YORK

Copyright © 2016 Disney Enterprises, Inc. All rights reserved. Published in the United States by Golden Books, an imprint of Random House Children's Books, a division of Penguin Random House LLC, 1745 Broadway, New York, NY 10019, and in Canada by Penguin Random House Canada Limited, Toronto. Golden Books, A Golden Book, A Big Golden Book, the G colophon, and the distinctive gold spine are registered trademarks of Penguin Random House LLC.
randomhousekids.com
ISBN 978-0-7364-3562-8
Printed in the United States of America
10 9 8 7 6 5 4 3 2 1

One evening, Kristoff was visiting Bulda and the rest of the trolls in Troll Valley while Grand Pabbie was away. They were roasting mushrooms when one of Bulda's crystals started to flicker.

"Oh!" she said, surprised. "My favorite crystal is going dark! Grand Pabbie gave this to me when you came to live with us, Kristoff. It reminds me of how perfectly you fit into our family."

Bulda had given Kristoff and
Sven a home when they were young
and alone. Kristoff was grateful to
her for so much. He didn't like to
see her disappointed.

"How do you fix it?" he asked.

"All I know is that it must be taken somewhere and recharged by the next time the Northern Lights fade, or it will lose its magical glow forever," explained Bulda. "Grand Pabbie would know what to do if he were here."

"I'll take care of it," said Kristoff. "Sven and I will get started first thing tomorrow."

Kristoff and Sven set out early the next morning.
Their first stop was Arendelle. They found Anna, Elsa,
and Olaf in the castle library. Kristoff told them what had
happened and asked them for help.

"Of course!" cried Anna. "We're coming with you."

Elsa pulled a book about crystals from the shelf.

"Crystals can be recharged 'where lights wake the sky, where the sky touches the earth, and where waters run long,'" she read.

"Lights that wake the sky could be the Northern Lights, which Bulda mentioned," said Anna.

"Where the sky touches the earth could be a mountaintop," said Kristoff.

"And where waters run long could be the fjord by Oppalding Mountain!" exclaimed Anna.

The friends set out for Oppalding Mountain. After hiking all morning, they arrived at the top of a steep cliff.

"According to the map, we'll have to climb down the cliff," Anna said. "There's no other way."

Anna went first. Kristoff was next.
But Elsa had an idea. "I have an easier route," she said.

With a wave of her hands, Elsa used her magic to create an ice slide on the side of the cliff! She, Olaf, and Sven zoomed past Kristoff and Anna.

"Wheee!" cried Olaf.

A few hours later, the friends finally reached the top of Oppalding Mountain. But there was nothing at the summit except bare rock.

Kristoff looked around, puzzled. "I don't see any crystals. Do you think we went to the wrong mountain?"

The sun was beginning to set, so the group decided to stop and camp for the night.

"Maybe we'll have better luck in the morning," said Anna.

As the friends settled into their blankets, a
ribbon of glowing color spread across the night sky.
"I love it when the sky's awake," said Olaf,
sighing happily.

"But I've never seen the rocks glow," Olaf continued, gazing at the craggy overhang behind them.

Everyone turned around. Where light from the colored sky hit the rock, spots of red, green, yellow, and purple were glowing deep inside!

"Could those be crystals?" asked Elsa.

Kristoff took out his climbing ax, but Sven nudged him aside.

CRACK! CRACK! CRACK! Sven hit the rock with his antlers, and tiny fissures appeared.

"Maybe I can help," said Elsa. She used her powers to freeze the rock. Ice crept into the cracks, forcing them to open wider. Anna tried to wiggled her arm inside a crack, but the opening was too narrow.

"Kristoff, may I see Bulda's crystal?" asked Anna. She reached
into the rock again, holding Bulda's crystal close to the ones inside.
When they touched, Bulda's crystal began to glow!

Anna was sure she had saved the day, but Bulda's crystal started to fade.

"What happened?" asked Anna. "I thought we had completed the quest."

Discouraged, the group headed home.
They hadn't been able to recharge Bulda's
crystal, but they knew they had tried their best.
And everyone had to admit it had been an
exciting adventure!

When they arrived in Troll Valley, Bulda greeted them with hugs. "Welcome back!" she said.

"I'm sorry, Bulda," said Kristoff, "but we weren't able to recharge your crystal."

"This crystal can be finicky," said Bulda. "Let's take a look."

Anna placed the stone in Bulda's hands.

Suddenly, the crystal began to glow!

"You did it!" said Bulda. "You worked together, had fun, and supported each other as a family. That provided the special power the crystal needed to glow again."

"I get it!" Kristoff grinned. "But don't forget that we did it for you, because you're family, too."

They all agreed: family is one of the most powerful forces in the world.